EX LIBRIS
THIS BOOK BELONGS TO

VOLUME ONE

ROMAN MYTHS

FIONA MACDONALD

SCRIBBLERS

a SALARIYA *imprint*

Published in Great Britain in MMXX by
Scribblers, an imprint of
The Salariya Book Company Ltd
25 Marlborough Place,
Brighton BN1 1UB
www.salariya.com

HB ISBN-13: 978-1-912904-78-5

3 5 7 9 8 6 4 2 1

A CIP catalogue record for this book
is available from the British Library.

Printed and bound in China.

Illustrations by:

Patrick Brooks
The Golden Chair
Pomona and Vertumnus
Hercules and the Giant Who Spat Fire

Serena Lombardo
The Adventures of Aeneas Part One
The Adventures of Aeneas Part Two
Aeneas in the Underworld
Romulus and Remus
Arethusa – The Girl Who Gave Water

Visit
www.salariya.com
for our online catalogue and
free fun stuff.

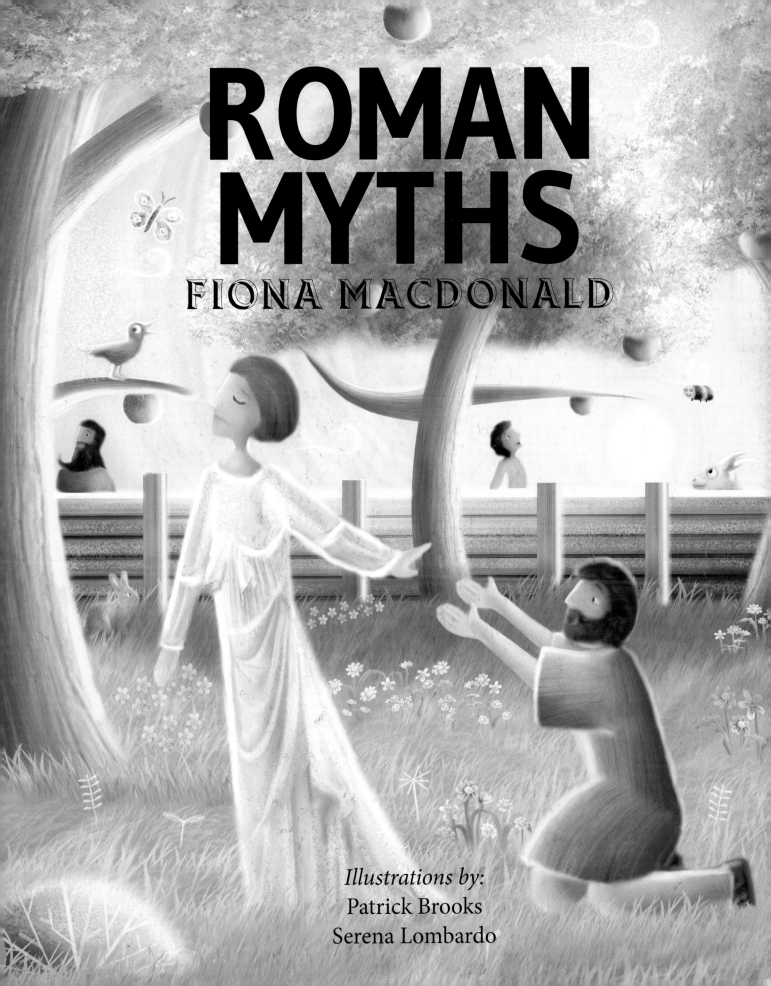

ROMAN MYTHS

FIONA MACDONALD

Illustrations by:

Patrick Brooks

Serena Lombardo

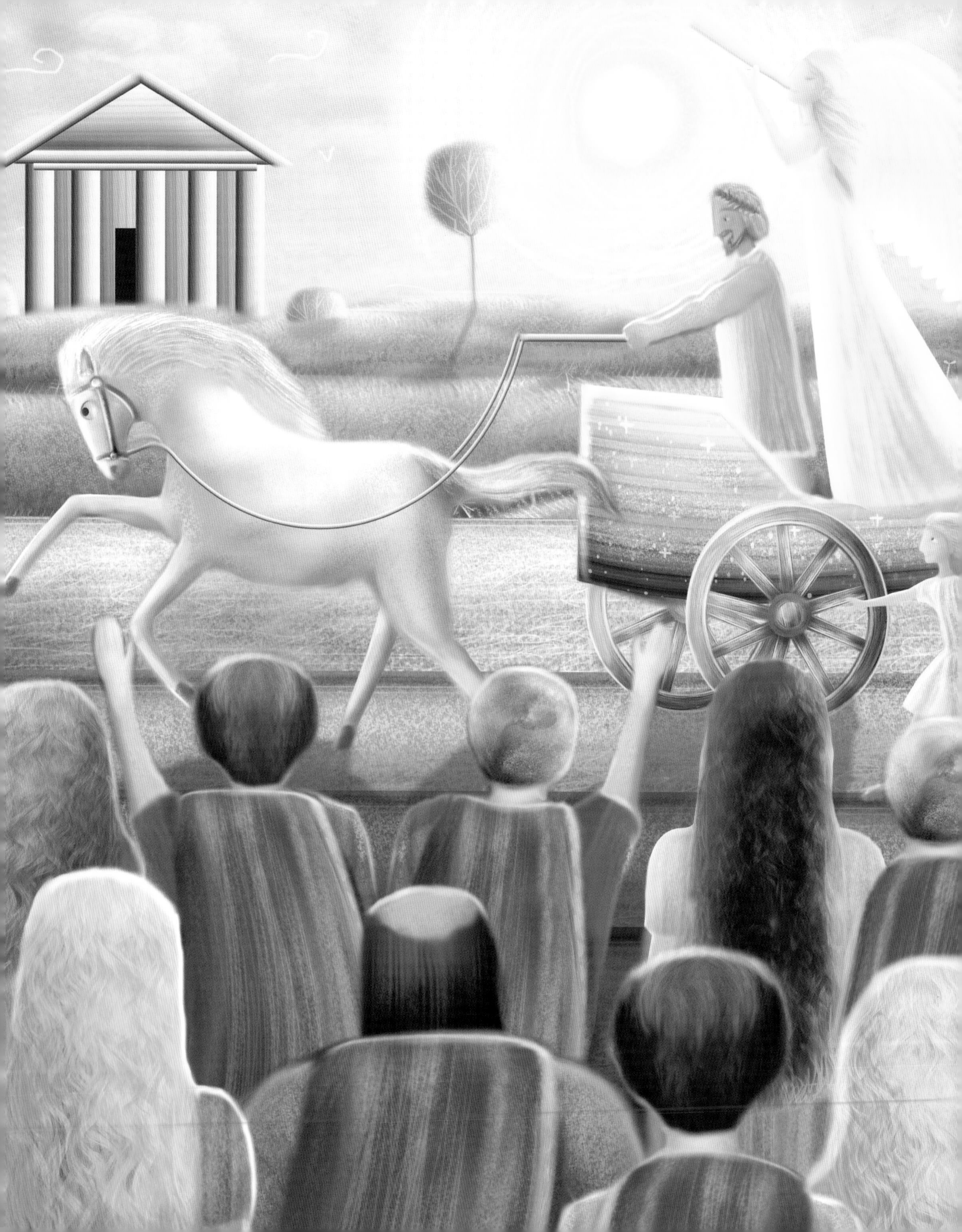

CONTENTS

INTRODUCTION

This book recounts some of the best-known myths and legends from Ancient Rome. They have all been enjoyed for over 2,000 years. When you read them, you'll be entering into the thoughts and hopes and fears and dreams of people who lived when Rome was a great city, with fantastic temples and palaces, when Roman engineers devised great new inventions, and when Roman army legions patrolled the frontiers of an empire that stretched from Scotland to Syria.

Reading myths from any past civilisation, including Rome and its empire, is like time-travel for the mind. We can see and touch the remains of buildings and earthworks that the Romans left behind; myths and legends help us learn what those Roman builders (and their parents and wives and slaves and children) were thinking.

Why do we (and other peoples) tell stories? For all sorts of reasons. Myths and legends (traditional tales that may or may not be true) are the world's oldest tales. They have survived because they are entertaining, funny, scary, inspiring and sad. But much more than that: myths and legends carry a message. They are stories with a meaning. They helped people in the past, and may still help us today, to make sense of the world.

Roman myths and legends also tell the story of a particular group of people: refugees from a glorious city destroyed by war. They describe the heroism of the survivors, and how they fought against all kinds of dangers to find a new place to settle. There, they created a wonderful new civilisation. It still shapes our language and literature. We can still admire it today.

THE ADVENTURES OF AENEAS

PART ONE

It was an appalling sight. The mighty city of Troy invaded, shattered, in flames. Bodies filled the streets; the stench of death hung in the air. Clouds of black smoke from Troy's famous tall buildings billowed and swirled all around, threatening to choke the few survivors.

There were only a few of those, and a sorry lot they were. So many brave Trojan fighters had been killed, defending their homes and families from Greek attack. So many weeping Trojan women and children had been led away, to be sold as

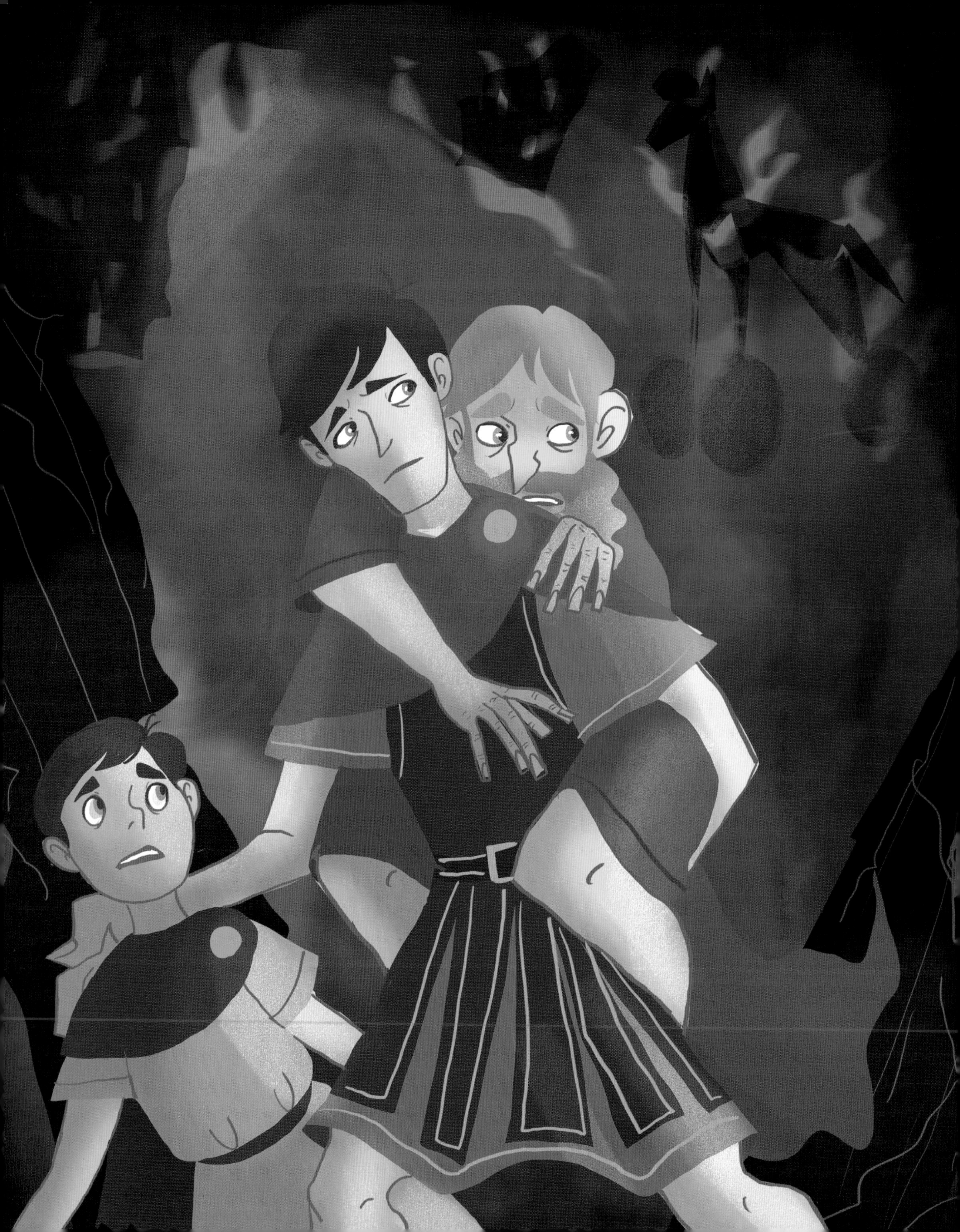

slaves. King Priam of Troy had been murdered, and his warrior sons lay dead in battle. Even scary priestess Cassandra (who had warned of Troy's destruction) was now the captive of Greek King Agamemnon.

Among all the royal family of Troy, only Prince Aeneas survived. He had fought alongside his brothers and comrades, and seen them die. He was not the best or bravest of them, and yet he had been spared. Why, the survivors asked, was Aeneas still alive? And, as Aeneas struggled out of the city, carrying his aged father on his back and clasping his little son by the hand, he asked himself the same question.

'Why me? What is my duty?'

The answer was simple. That is, if Aeneas and the survivors believed messages sent by their gods. Aeneas was a man with a mission. His task was to lead the survivors from Troy to a new homeland, and build another great city there. One day,

Aeneas's city would be as rich and splendid as Troy itself, or maybe even better.

Aeneas was brave and tough; loyal, determined and pious; the best man among the survivors. The gods would help him, especially goddess Venus. Aeneas was one of her favourites. Some people said that she, not a human woman, was Aeneas's mother.

Even with the gods' help, dangers still faced them. Where to go? How to get there? And what dangers lay in wait on the way?

Their first move was clear. They must get away from Troy. Aeneas led the survivors down to the shore, still carrying his father and holding tight to his son. Everyone could still see and smell their once-beautiful city burning in the distance.

Wasting no time, Aeneas gave orders to get together a fleet of 20 ships. By spring, they were ready. The survivors clambered aboard, grabbed the oars and hoisted the sails. They headed north towards Thrace where Trojan merchants often traded. Should they build their new city here?

But look! On the shore! Are we dreaming? See! A bush, on fire!

The flames leaped up, but the bush was not burned, although dark blood dripped from its leaves. Stranger still, it spoke to them, urgently, pleading.

The voice belonged to Polydorus, one of dead King Priam's sons.

'Go away! Get out! Don't build here! This is cursed land! I came here carrying gold, and the king had me murdered. Now I'm trapped in this bush until someone says prayers to set my spirit free. Do that, Aeneas, then sail south! And quickly!'

Aeneas did as he was told. He held a solemn

funeral for Polydorus, then led the Trojans back to the ships and far out to sea.

Their next landfall was on Delos, a magic, floating island.

'I must consult the oracle here,' said Aeneas. 'It speaks with Apollo's voice. The god will guide me.'

Eerily, scarily, as if from another world, the oracle moaned, 'Go to your first homeland!'

Aeneas had his answer. But what did it mean? Confused and disappointed, he turned to his father.

'Perhaps we should head for the isle of Crete?', suggested the old man. 'Legends say that long ago the Trojans lived there.'

And that is what they did. And it was a failure. Their new houses fell down, their crops died in the fields and they all became ill.

'We can't stay here,' said Aeneas. 'We'll die! We must go back to the oracle and get another answer.'

The survivors muttered and grumbled. Aeneas was worried too. That night, he couldn't sleep. As he tossed and turned, feeling wretched, he thought he saw something in the darkness. What was it? A shape! A human? No, a little god. Two gods! The kindly Penates, who guarded homes and families.

In soft, low, helpful voices they whispered: 'Go west, Aeneas! To the Hesperides. To the land of the setting sun!'

They had been at sea now for several days and water was running low. The lookout yelled: 'Over there! Some rocks! Maybe it's an island?!'

'Steer towards it!' ordered Aeneas.

They landed on the shore. Yes, there was fresh water, but there was also something else. Flesh-eating Harpies! Lots of them! Huge, looming, flapping, cawing, wondrous. Beautiful but also utterly foul.

Part women, part bird, they flocked around the survivors, snatching the food they had spread on the sand and (disgusting!) using the table as a toilet. Their beaks and claws were razor sharp; their voices were menacing.

Their leader spoke. 'You're not welcome here, Aeneas. Go away! Go away, and face new dangers! They're waiting for you, you'll see!'

Then, with a grim cackle, she rose into the air and flapped horribly away.

Another long sea voyage. No, many of them. So many, the survivors were losing count. All round the coast of Greece, then north and west towards Albania. There, they landed and met another refugee from Troy, Prince Helenus.

Helenus could see into the future. He did not have good news to share.

'Oh Aeneas!' he cried. 'Beware! Beware! So many

dangers lay ahead. I can't say that you'll survive them. But if you do, here's how you'll know that you have reached your new homeland. You'll see a fat white sow with thirty piglets, resting under an oak tree.'

'But before you get there, take this advice.' He looked suddenly really serious. 'Stay away from Scylla and Charybdis' – 'Who? What?' thought Aeneas – 'and take care, very great care, not to offend the goddess Juno.'

Helenus knew that Juno had just quarrelled with Aeneas's mother, Venus. The two goddesses were enemies; now Juno was bound to be hostile to Aeneas, as well.

They were back at sea, sailing through the narrow channel between Italy and the nearby island of Sicily. The waters were choppy and swirling; strangely rough for the time of year. A roaring sound grew louder every minute. Then suddenly, the prows of the boats spun round, as if dragged by a giant hand from deep underwater. It was Charybdis, the killer whirlpool!

'Man the oars!' Aeneas yelled. 'Everyone! All of you! Row for your lives!'

It was a narrow escape, but they survived. And then, to be extra careful, the helmsman steered the fleet as far away from the whirlpool as he could, close to the opposite shore.

Crunch! Bump! Grind! Aeneas's boat swayed and jolted as its hull ran into something unseen and unexpected. Only good luck, or the gods, stopped everyone on board being thrown overboard and drowned.

It was another monster! Scylla-with-the-Sharp-Teeth, Charybdis's constant companion. A deadly cluster of jagged rocks, she lay in wait out of sight just below the water's surface, ready to catch unwary ships and sailors and devour them.

Another brush with death. But another survival. Aeneas's ship floated safely off Scylla's rocks at the next high tide. And sailed on.

By now, they were nearing the western land, the Hesperides. But their troubles were not over. Exhausted, they came ashore to rest on the coast of Sicily. It was a gloomy, threatening spot. Wild waves crashed on the beach and behind them loomed a grumbling, belching volcano. From time to time, flames leapt high into the sky from the volcano's mouth, and clouds of red-hot ash rained down, threatening to choke and burn them.

'Perhaps the next bay will be better?' said Aeneas. 'Let's try.'

They landed. And soon found that they were not alone. Wild-eyed, dressed in rags, half-crazed, but delighted to see them, a castaway Greek sailor staggered across the sand.

'Take me away from here,' he begged. 'It's not

safe! Let me tell you…! They're awful…!'

Aeneas offered the sailor food and drink, and sat down to listen to his story.

'There are terrible creatures here!' exclaimed the sailor. 'Cyclops! Frightful, man-eating giants, with just one eye in the middle of their forehead. They lumber about armed with huge stone clubs, ready to bash your brains out.'

'And…' he shuddered, 'They like to go hunting for humans!'

Aeneas stretched out a comforting hand and patted the sailor on the shoulder.

'My friend,' he said gently. 'Your time alone on the beach has made you mad. Cyclops are not real. They only exist in myths and legends…'

He had hardly finished speaking when giant roars and bellows echoed round the mountain slopes behind them, and heavy footfalls made the earth tremble.

Aeneas leapt to his feet. 'What's that?! What's that!'

Beneath his sunburn, the sailor turned pale.

'Cyclops!' he gasped. 'They're coming to get us! Run! Run! Run!'

THE ADVENTURES OF AENEAS

PART TWO

Onwards, ever onwards, still sailing west. Exhausted by old age and long years of travel, Aeneas's father died. They buried him on Sicily, then headed out to sea again. But a terrible storm, sent by jealous goddess Juno, drove them off course. Death now seemed certain.

But Venus begged Neptune, god of the oceans, to save Aeneas, and Neptune calmed the waves. More dead than alive, the survivors were washed ashore in Libya, on the north coast of Africa.

Were more monsters waiting? No! Their welcome could not have been kinder. They were taken to the fine new city of Carthage, to meet its queen, Dido. Herself a refugee, she took pity on the bedraggled Trojans, gave them food and drink, found them lodgings, and provided wood so their ships could be repaired.

And Aeneas? Ah, Aeneas. A handsome prince from overseas. Dido was young, beautiful and lonely. She fell in love with him.

Their love affair continued for a whole happy year. Dido wanted it to last forever. But, as we know, Aeneas was a man with a mission. He could not forget it, and Jupiter, king of the gods, would not let him neglect his duty. In fact, he sent messenger god Mercury to remind him.

Sadly, sternly, Aeneas said goodbye to Dido for ever and sailed away.

And Dido? Heartbroken, and angry with Aeneas

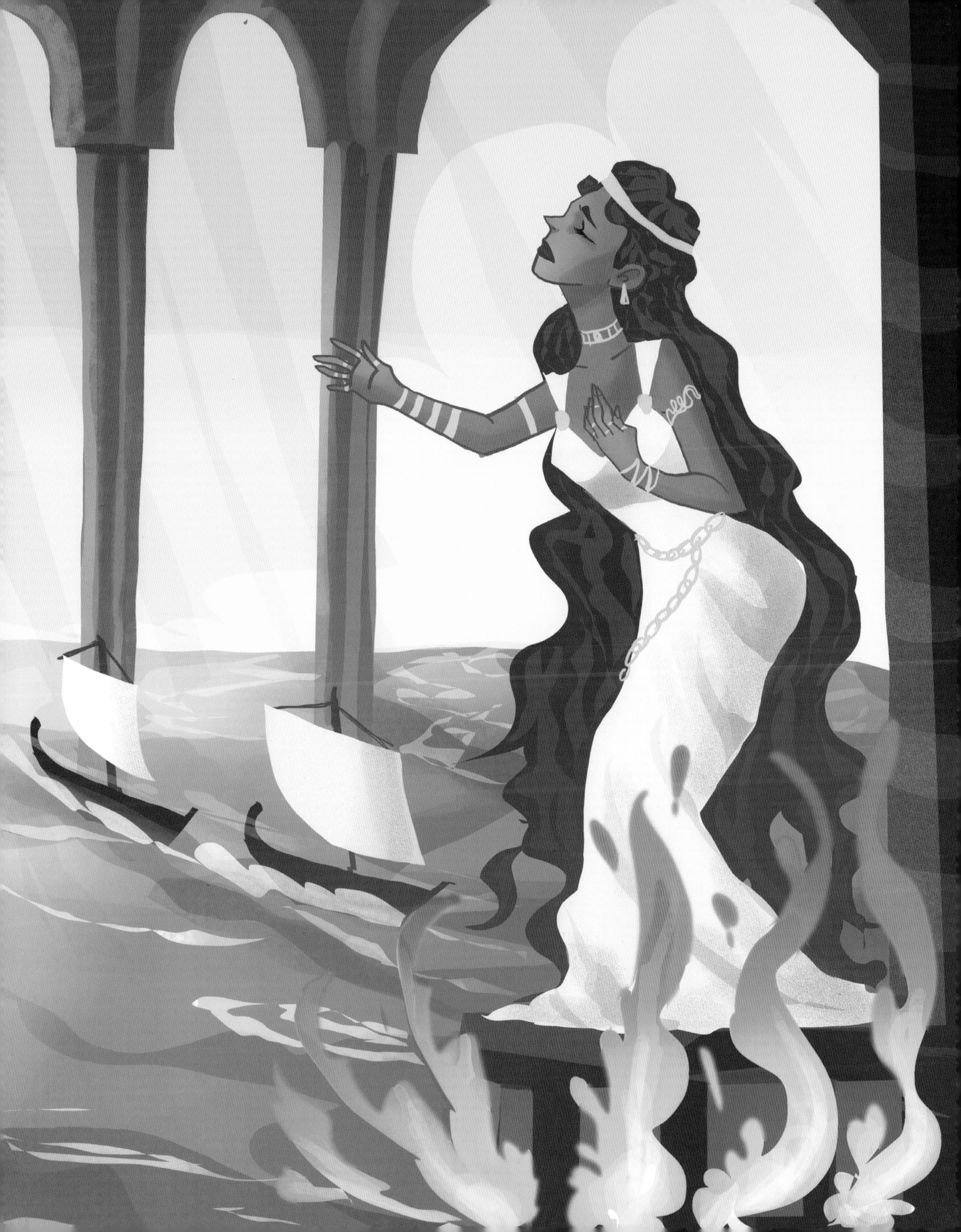

and his gods, she built a splendid funeral bonfire
and threw herself into the flames.

Heading north once more, Aeneas and the
survivors went back to Sicily, to say prayers and
hold funeral games to honour the memory of his
father's death. His father's ghost still haunted the
place: plaintive, lonely.

'Come to visit me in the Underworld,' the ghost
pleaded. 'I long to see you once more, and I have
so much to tell you.'

The sight of the
ghost made the
Trojans unhappy,
especially the women.

'Will our journey
never end?' they
asked. 'We're growing
old and tired.'

Goddess Juno heard them, and sent a messenger: Iris, the rainbow. She gave the women an idea. Secretly, they set fire to Aeneas's fleet. Now there would be no more voyaging! The Trojans would settle here, in Sicily.

Aeneas was appalled. How could he lead the Trojans to their proper new homeland? Urgently, he prayed:

'Jupiter! Lord of the skies! Help me! Help me!'

With a rumble of thunder and a lightning flash, the heavens opened and rain poured down in torrents. The fires went out. Only four ships had been damaged. The others survived.

'You can stay here if you want,' said Aeneas to the women. 'But I'm sailing on. And any man who wants to build a new Troy must come with me!'

Success often comes at a price. And the price for the next safe voyage was a human sacrifice, demanded by the god Neptune. 'One of your sailors must die,' he said. 'I choose Palinurus, your helmsman. I'll send the god of sleep to make him drowsy, and he'll fall overboard.'

Italy! At last! At last! Aeneas and his faithful troop of Trojans had not yet reached their new homeland, but they were drawing near.

The sea-stained ships sailed on, until they came to the mouth of the wide River Tiber. With beating heart, and prayers to Venus, Aeneas guided their ships upstream. The Trojans gazed around half fearful, half delighted. Was this it? The site of their new city? Was this their promised land?

If it was, it was not empty. People were already living here. Waiting to greet them stood elderly, dignified King Latinus, and his beautiful daughter Lavinia. Was it just a trick of the light, or did magic flames surround her hair?

The first meeting was friendly. King Latinus was

generous. His men helped the Trojans unload their ships. Lavinia smiled kindly, and watched them. Behind her, in the forest, a mother pig and her babies squealed and grunted.

After so many years, and such a long journey, and deaths and dangers and disasters, the refugee Trojans had found peace at last. They would build a new city here. It would have the new name of Rome, but it would grow great and powerful. A new Troy, just as glorious as the old. Already, to the Trojans, the place seemed like home.

But the gods never rest, especially the jealous ones. Already, Juno was summoning a hateful, spiteful Fury to pour anger and suspicion into the hearts of King Latinus's people. Urged on by the Fury, local hero Turnus challenged Aeneas to a duel.

'How dare you take our land?' he roared. 'We don't want you here!'

'It is my destiny,' said Aeneas. 'My mother,

Goddess Venus, has guided me.'

And so there was war, and death, as brave men died. But at long last, brave, determined Aeneas killed Turnus and ruled old Latinus's kingdom, with flame-haired Lavinia as his queen beside him, and Venus keeping watch from the skies.

The epic tale of Aeneas is full of fantastic adventures. But it also asks serious questions that still concern the world today. Should all brave warriors be honoured as heroes, whichever side they fight for? Should all wars be mourned, for the sufferings they cause? And where can refugees find shelter as they flee from devastated cities?

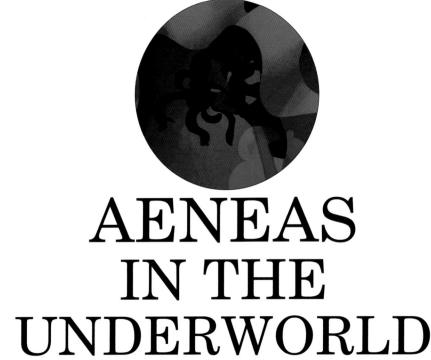

AENEAS
IN THE
UNDERWORLD

Do you remember how Aeneas's father died before the Trojans had reached the promised land of Latium? And how his pale ghost appeared to Aeneas, begging him to visit the land of the dead? Aeneas was always pious: respectful of his ancestors and his gods. The thought of the Underworld made him tremble with horror, but he knew he must do his duty. And so, shortly after he landed on the shores of Italy, he left the other Trojans and climbed a steep, forbidding mountain, right up to her cave, to find her...

Her? Who was she? The Sibyl. A priestess. A seer into the future. A very scary old woman. An oracle of the god Apollo. She lived all alone in a dark and gloomy cavern, deep inside the mountain. Every sound there echoed round and round the rocks, so they said that the cave had a hundred voices. All came from great Apollo himself.

The Sybil was expecting Aeneas's visit. She was waiting for him at the entrance to the cave.

'It is time,' she said. 'Time to consult the god. Time to say your prayers.'

All of a sudden she grew taller. She shook all over, clutching her chest, heaving and gasping. As she reeled and tottered, her long grey hair flew around her head like snakes. Her eyes glowed with fire. Even the dark and dirty rags she was dressed in seemed to come alive.

The god was speaking. His message was grim.

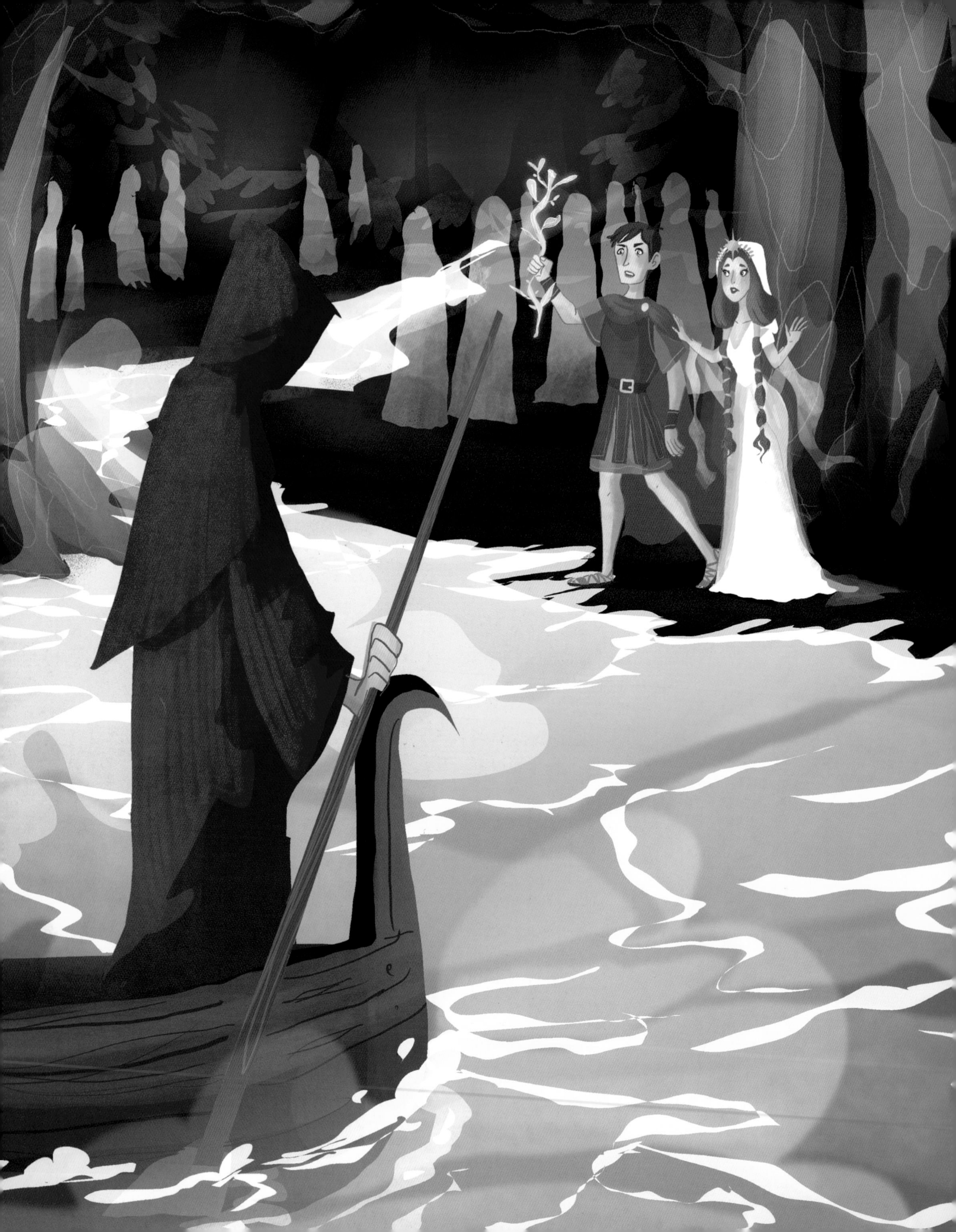

'Aeneas, you have faced many dangers, and fought against them bravely. But your troubles are not over. I see the River Tiber, where you will build your new city, foaming with blood. I see wars, wars, wars against rivals and neighbours. I see jealous Juno plotting to harm you. But I also see a glorious future, if you can fight and endure.'

At last, the Sibyl lay still. The power had left her. She was exhausted. Aeneas tried to calm his racing thoughts and pounding heart.

'Wise Sibyl,' he cried. 'Have pity on me, and on my father. He wants to see me just once more, and give me advice. Lead me to him, I beg you.'

The Sibyl looked at him sternly.

'Are you man enough for this? Is there love and courage in your heart? If so, then yes, I will. But remember this warning: entering the Underworld is easy. Returning is the problem!

'And before we set out, you must prove yourself. Somewhere on my mountain, you will find a tree branch of gleaming gold. Find it. Bring it here. Then we will go.'

It took time, but Venus sent twin doves – her favourites, symbols of love – to guide Aeneas. With a mixture of eagerness and dread he carried the branch to the Sibyl. Together they prepared a bloody sacrifice to please the gods of the Underworld; killing black sheep and cows, and pouring out their blood. An angry Sun rose, red and smouldering.

'Now is the time for courage!' cried the Sibyl. Together, they plunged into the darkness of death.

It was cold. Deadly cold. Sunless and sad. Death was surrounded by his helpers: Famine, Plague, Old Age, Poverty, Sickness, Sleep and Fear. They stretched out clammy, claw-like hands to grab Aeneas, but the Sibyl protected him. Grief and Care sat weeping and sobbing nearby. Guilt was there too, and Fury and Strife.

Further down, the Tree of False Dreams sheltered nightmare creatures: snake-headed Gorgons (whose glance turned men to stone), triple-bodied Gethion, whose legs fused together in a dragon's poisonous tail, the Chimera (a giant bird-snake-goat that spat fire), and many, many more.

Next, the Sibyl led Aeneas to the swirling, steaming Styx; the river of Dreadful Night, the river of No Return. The smell from its pitch-black waters was disgusting. A grim, surly, grey-bearded ferryman, the god Charon, stood in the shadows, pushing away hundreds, or perhaps thousands, of pale, pitiful ghosts who were trying to climb in to his murky boat.

'Those are the spirits of good people,' said the Sibyl. 'Young boys and girls, brave warriors, kind fathers, hard-working mothers. All have died, but have not yet been buried. No funeral prayers have been said for them. So they cannot cross the river. They cannot rest in peace.

'But we must board Charon's boat, if you dare.
The golden branch will be our passport. And we'll
meet more monsters on the other side.'

It bayed. It howled. It towered over them. Three
angry mouths with slavering jaws and snarling
teeth threatened to devour them. Hastily, the Sybil

threw some meat, dripping with a sleeping potion, towards Cerberus, guard-dog at the gates of hell. He wolfed it down, and sank, snoring, into a deep slumber.

'Come on. Quickly!' hissed the Sibyl. Aeneas followed her.

So much to see! Aeneas looked in bewilderment as the Sibyl hurried him along. Here were the spirits of new-born babies, and men and women who had killed themselves or been unjustly killed. There, in the Fields of Mourning, were the weeping spirits of those who died for love. And here is Dido, the beautiful queen. Aeneas rushed towards her, but angrily she turned her back on him, and hurried away.

Shaken and sorrowful, Aeneas followed the Sibyl once more, past dead Trojan princes; past the ghosts of his comrades and enemies, killed in war. Then past a massive fortress on the edge of a bottomless chasm. The pit of Tartarus! Eternal place of punishment for the wicked. The home of the damned. Thunder crashed overhead. Blood-curdling screams rang out. Aeneas shuddered. He felt sick with fear.

He left the Golden Branch as an offering to Pluto and Proserpina, king and queen of the Underworld, then hurried to where the Sibyl stood beckoning. Here, for the first time in the Underworld, there was sunshine and green grass and trees and flowers. And music and dancing and sports and science and poetry. In the distance, he could see dreamy, sleepy Lethe, the river of forgetfulness, where spirits were washed free of past troubles, ready to be re-born.

'The Elysian Fields,' said the Sibyl. 'Home of the blessed. Resting place for people who have lived good lives, and especially for heroes. See, Aeneas, see! Your father approaches.'

Delighted, but with tears pouring down his cheeks, Aeneas rushed to embrace his father. But his eager arms felt nothing but themselves.

The Sibyl said gently, 'This is the land of spirits, of winged dreams.'

The ghost of Aeneas's father spoke.

'My son! My son! I have longed for this moment! I saw the dangers you faced to lead the Trojans to a new homeland. And I admire your bravery. Now let me tell you how your children and your children's children for hundreds of years will rule the glorious city of Rome. It will be home to heroes. Its empire will reach to the ends of the earth. Now, listen to my advice…'

His father had gone. Aeneas was weary. His head was heavy. His limbs felt like lead. His heart ached; he knew he would never, ever see his father again. Should he, too, stay here, in the land of the dead and learn to forget the living? It would be so easy, to let his eyelids close and never wake up again.

The Sibyl spoke sharply. 'Come on, Aeneas! Duty calls!'

Remembering all he had fought for, Aeneas followed her. Back into the daylight. Back to join the living. Back to a future Rome.

ROMULUS AND REMUS

A city needs a story of how it began. And the bigger and stronger a city, the more amazing that story needs to be. This is the story that the Romans told themselves about how their city was founded, they said around 754 BC.

Archaeology tells us that people were living in the Seven Hills region where Rome now stands for hundreds of years before then. Perhaps the Romans knew that; perhaps they did not. It doesn't really matter. What was important to them was to link their great city of Rome and its empire with famous Roman heroes from the past and with mighty Roman gods...

A lone wolf. A savage wolf. A running wolf. A wild wolf. Wolves are cruel, uncivilised outsiders preying on animals and people. And yet, and yet... if it hadn't been for a mother wolf who rescued two helpless human babies, the whole history of Rome might have been very, very different.

Let's begin at the beginning. Hundreds of years after hero Aeneas landed in Italy, his descendants ruled the city of Alba Longa. Numitor, who was king there, had a younger brother, Amulius, and the two were bitter rivals. Amulius plotted and threw Numitor off the throne. Now he was king of Alba Longa. He was rich. He was powerful.

'So far, so good!' thought Amulius. 'But Numitor's sons and grandsons will surely seek revenge. They'll try to win back power. So I'll have them all killed! And I'll send Numitor's daughter to the goddess Vesta's temple. Vesta's priestesses must not marry or have children. If old Numitor's daughter breaks that rule, she'll be buried alive.'

The Alba Longa citizens heard Amulius and were afraid. But the gods heard him too, and decided that hero Aeneas's family should survive. No one knows quite how it happened, though most said that Mars, god of war, was the father, but old King Numitor's daughter gave birth to twins: two fine and healthy boys.

King Amulius was furious. 'Those babies must die!' he raged.

He told his servants to toss the twins into the River Tiber that flowed close by. 'That way, it will be the gods who decide their fate,' Amulius said. 'Perhaps they'll float, perhaps they'll drown. But I won't be guilty.'

'And', he added, snarling, 'I won't kill their mother, either, but shut her up in prison and throw away the key.'

Tiberinus, the river god, was listening. 'I'll save those boys!' he decided. So he calmed the river waters and sent gentle waves to carry the twins to the river bank, where a fig tree stretched out its tangle of roots to catch them.

There (a further wonder!) they were found by a mother wolf. Picking them up very gently by the scruff of the neck, she carried them to her lair, a cave under one of the Seven Hills. She licked them dry, fed them just like puppies, washed them, curled herself round them to keep them warm, and sprang to her feet to guard them whenever she heard footsteps of sheep or shepherds nearby.

But babies are noisy; even twins descended from heroes and guarded by the gods. So, one day, shepherd Faustulus heard them laughing and crying as he was searching for a lost sheep. He tracked them down to the cave (the mother wolf was out hunting) and carried them home to his wife. They had no children, and so were delighted to have a family at last. They cared for the twins, now named Romulus and Remus, until they grew up, teaching them how to care for sheep and do all kinds of useful jobs around the farm. However, they did not tell the twins how they found them, or where they came from.

By the time Romulus and Remus were teenagers, it was clear that they were not like other boys. They were bolder, stronger and much more determined. They joined the local gang of youths that played sports together and sometimes stole cattle from neighbouring tribes.

'Troublemakers!' said some villagers. 'Future leaders!' said the others. And that was true.

On one of their raids, the twins' gang found themselves caught up in a fight between supporters of Amulius and old King Numitor. Remus was captured and marched off to Alba Longa. As soon as Numitor saw him, he began to wonder.

'After all these years? Are my old eyes deceiving me? They remind me so much of my daughter. I was sure the twins had drowned in the river.'

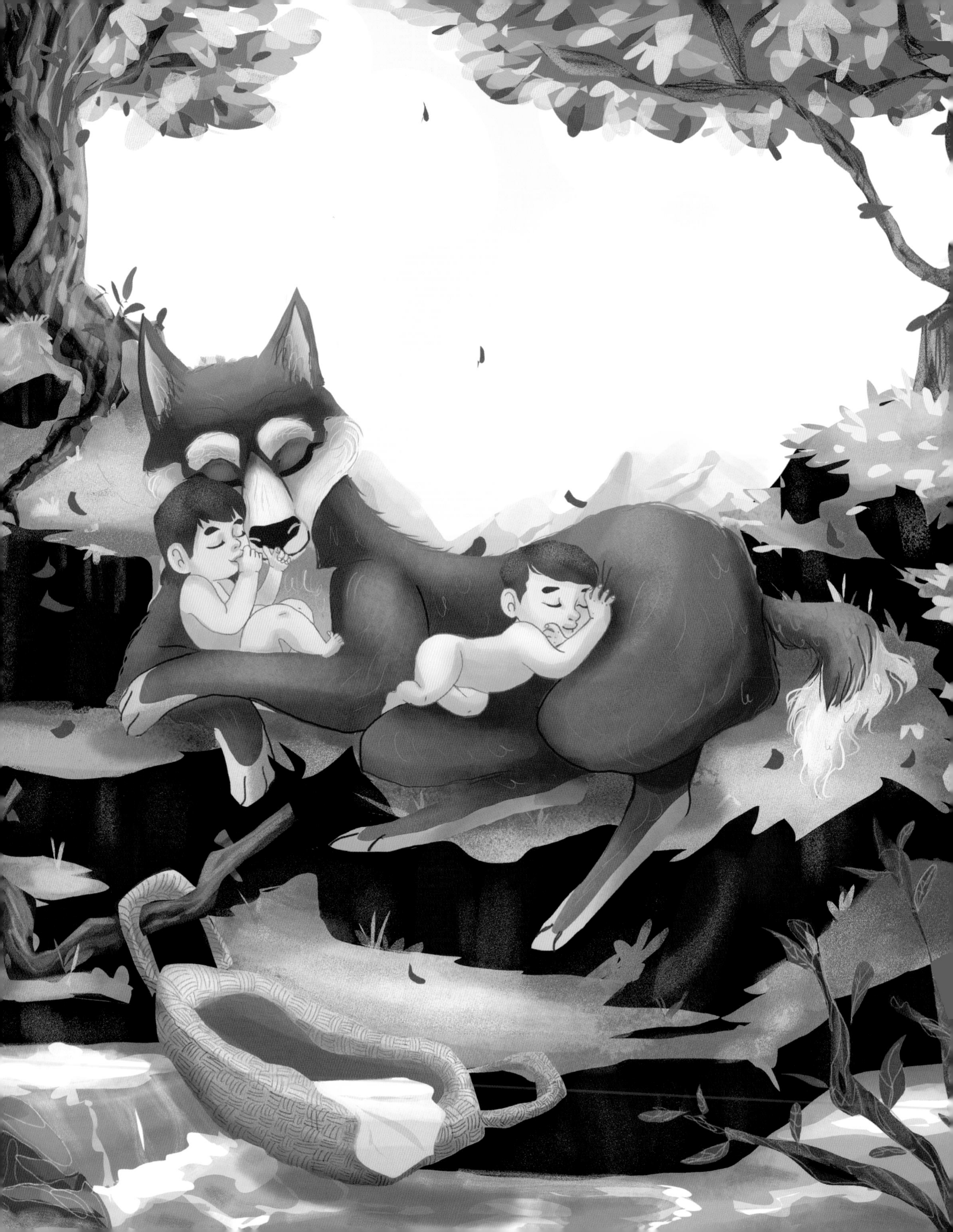

Meanwhile, Romulus and his gang had got together with other keen young fighters. They hurried to Alba Longa to rescue Remus. Then they joined forces with Numitor, now convinced that the boys were his grandsons. After a bloody battle, Amulius was killed. Numitor became king of Alba Longa once again and the twins' mother was set free.

The story of their royal birth and their magical rescue made Romulus and Remus even more certain that an exciting future lay ahead of them. They decided to build their own city. It would grow rich and powerful and be the home of a great civilisation. It would rule all the known world. And its fame would live for ever.

Together, the twins admired the wide River Tiber (and gave thanks to its god for saving them). Together, they explored the Seven Hills. Romulus spoke first. 'I think we should start building on the Palatine Hill. That's where the wolf's lair was. This is the site of our first home!'

Remus shook his head. 'No! The Aventine Hill would be better. Much better. I'm certain!'

It was the start of a dreadful quarrel. How to make peace, and be friends again?

At long last, they agreed. 'We owe our lives to the gods,' they said together. 'Now let's ask them to help us decide where to build. We'll look for the messages they send in nature. We'll each go to our chosen hill and then wait for a sign from the heavens.'

'OK, brother?'

'You've got a deal!'

And they walked off in opposite directions.

Remus saw them first. Six birds, swooping and wheeling in formation round and round his hill.

Then Romulus saw them. Twelve birds this time.

Fluttering and flapping, almost as if they were dancing in the sky.

'The gods spoke to me first!' cried Remus.

'But my message was stronger!' Romulus argued back. 'I win!'

'No you don't! No you don't!' yelled Remus, and strode away, in fury.

Many months later, Romulus leaned back on his shovel and heaved a sigh of relief. Already, the trenches he and his men had dug marked out the boundaries of his city. Now they were starting to build a good strong wall. Next, there would be houses and temples and shops...

'Ha!' Remus strolled up, scoffing. 'Still hard at work? Serves you right for choosing such a difficult place for your city. I told you – remember, I TOLD you – that my hill would have been better.'

He walked away, then, all of a sudden, turned round and raced towards the partly-built wall. With a huge leap, he cleared it, and landed, laughing and jeering, on the other side.

'Who's going to be afraid of this?' he sniggered. 'Afraid of a little baby wall?!'

Romulus was outraged. How dare Remus make him look a fool in front of all his workmen? And how dare Remus threaten to bring a curse down on his new city of Rome? Everyone knew that walls were protected by the gods. If you damaged them, or mocked them, there was only one punishment!

Romulus then picked up his spade and killed his twin brother.

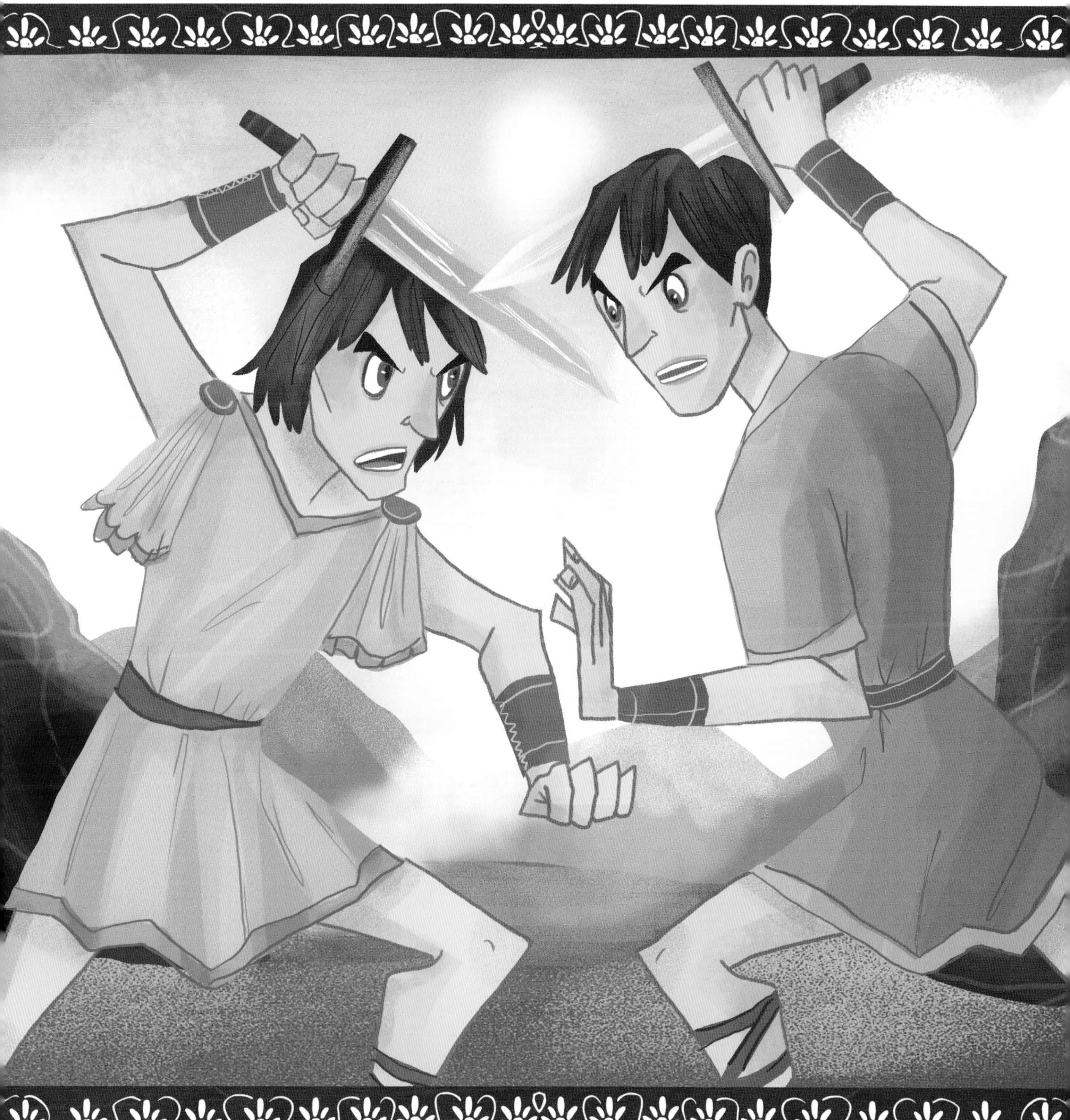

THE GOLDEN CHAIR

All the gods were good-looking. But then, one fine day, the queen of the gods – proud, beautiful Juno – gave birth to a son who looked nothing like a god. Or a prince. Or even a handsome human. Just a small, very plain and rather sickly baby. And he cried and cried, all the time. Instead of being happy, Juno felt angry and ashamed. After just one disgusted glance, she picked up her baby and threw him away!

It was a long way down from the top of Mount Olympus where Juno sat on her throne. The poor baby tumbled through the air, twisting and turning all day and all night long. Then he landed with a splash in deep sea water. He was lucky: he survived. But one of his legs was broken.

Down under the waves, the baby kept on falling. He fell until he reached the bottom of the sea; dizzy, exhausted, still crying. But then, more good luck! A sea goddess, Thetis, found him and took him to her underwater home. There she cared for him, with love and kindness.

Thanks to Thetis, the baby, whose name was Vulcan, grew up to be healthy and happy. He was never going to be handsome, but he was strong and clever. His broken leg remained crooked, so he walked with a limp on dry land. But that didn't stop him doing anything he wanted.

The sea and the seashore were great places for a child. There was so much to explore and discover. Vulcan played with sea-creatures (dolphins were his favourite); he collected pearls and shells and pebbles. He found a fire left by fishermen and discovered how to make it grow hotter. He did experiments, with rocks, and found that some of them contained precious metals: silver and gold! Later, he found rocks that contained useful iron.

As well as smelting metals, Vulcan discovered how to shape them into all kinds of useful and beautiful objects, from delicate gold jewellery to heavy iron weapons and tools. Later, the Romans honoured him as the inventor of metalwork, and the world's best blacksmith.

As a grown man, Vulcan moved away from the sea to a blacksmith's forge on dry land. But he always remembered Thetis and the care she had shown him, and he liked to make her beautiful things to show his gratitude.

The gift Thetis liked best was a lovely, delicate necklace of silver and precious stones. She was so pleased with it that she wore it on her next visit to the home of the gods on Mount Olympus. Proud

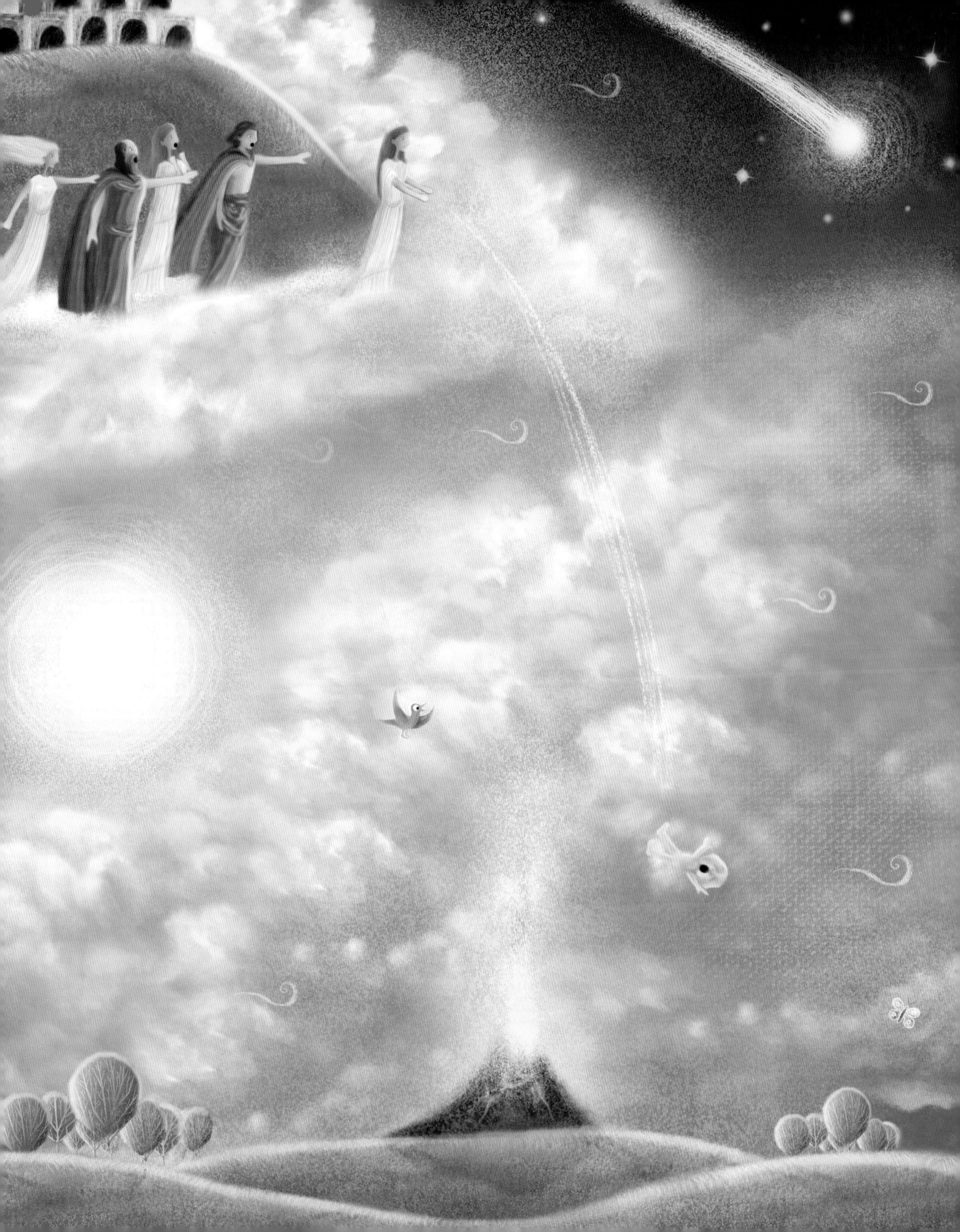

Juno was there, of course, and as soon as she saw the necklace she became consumed with jealousy.

'I must have one like that,' she said. 'I want it straight away! Tell me, Thetis, I command you! Where did you get it? Who made it?'

Poor Thetis! She faced a very difficult choice. If she refused to tell, Juno might fly into one of her famous rages. But if Thetis revealed that she knew how Juno had thrown her son away, well, she could not bear to think about what might happen. Thetis mumbled something vague, and then made an excuse to leave Mount Olympus and return to her home under the sea.

Juno was suspicious. What was Thetis hiding? So she sent spies to follow her, and they soon found out about how Thetis had cared for Vulcan. They spied on Vulcan, too, and reported that he had a blacksmith's forge full of newly-invented tools, and a treasure chest full of exquisite jewellery.

For once, Juno did not lose her temper, or scream and shout, or cry. She dismissed her spies and then sat down to think about what she should do.

At last, she decided. She would invite – no, she would command – Vulcan to meet her on Mount Olympus.

Vulcan said no. 'I don't care what she wants,' he exclaimed. 'She threw me out when I was helpless. Why should I try to please her? She has never cared for me.'

He limped off to his blacksmith's forge and calmed himself down by hammering bars of red-hot iron. As he worked, a plan for revenge began to grow in his mind.

'Yes, that'll show her,' he muttered. 'That will serve her right!'

For the next few weeks Vulcan worked harder than he had ever done before. He was making a special chair: a gold and silver throne decorated with precious stones. It was magnificent. In fact, it was fit for a queen!

By special messenger, Vulcan sent the throne to Juno on Mount Olympus. She was absolutely delighted. 'It's wonderful!' she cried. 'Look how it gleams and sparkles! It's the perfect chair for the

queen of the gods. Now everyone will envy me!'
'Come here, gods and goddesses!' she called.
'Come and look at me. Come quickly, and
admire!'

With a royal flourish of her hand and swirl of her
lovely long skirts, Juno lowered herself gracefully
into the chair. But as the other gods arrived, the
chair began to shiver and shake. Hidden chains
sprang out and wrapped themselves around Juno.

Proud, jealous
Juno was trapped!
The queen
was powerless!
The other gods
giggled and
sniggered. Down
on Earth, in
his blacksmith's
workshop,
Vulcan laughed
with them.

POMONA
AND
VERTUMNUS

Pomona lived all by herself in a garden filled with trees. It was a delightful spot: cool and shady, with little streams and grassy paths bordered by wild flowers. A place of peace and also of plenty. The trees were laden with the most sumptuous fruit: ripe red cherries, pink and green apples, golden peaches and deep purple plums. Bushes, too, produced handfuls of sweet berries. And twisting vines were hung with bunches of luscious grapes.

Wild birds sang; shy deer tiptoed round the outside of the strong fence protecting the garden. Pomona was proud of that; she had built it herself. In the distance, Pomona sometimes thought she saw friendly spirits peering out from the woods or dashing across the fields. Sometimes she heard them calling to each other or laughing. But she did not want to join them. With her garden to love and care for, she was never lonely.

Pomona worked hard all day, every day, weeding, watering, planting new trees and pruning well-grown ones. It was her home, her job, her pleasure and her relaxation.

For Pomona, life was good. She was happy. She wished to live alone in her beautiful, peaceful garden for ever. But the gods had decided a different future for her. Pomona was young, she was kind, she was clever, she was beautiful. Surely, she should not hide herself and her garden knowledge away? Perhaps, the gods thought, Pomona was getting a little too independent? She looked after her garden in her own way. But really, it should obey the laws of the changing seasons, like the rest of the natural world.

To begin with, Venus, goddess of love, inspired two nature-spirits to fall in love with Pomona: Silvanus the rough, tough hunter (almost as bloodstained and shaggy as the wolves he chased in the forests) and Picus the shepherd (handsome, well-dressed, cheerful and so silly that his friends called him bird-brained). One after the other, they hurried to find Pomona in her garden. But she locked the gate and refused to let them in. She hid behind her trees until Silvanus wearied of running round outside the fence trying to find her. And when Picus came, Pomona threw buckets of cold water from her garden stream all over him.

'Hmm,' said Venus. 'This is going to be more difficult than I imagined. But wait, I have an idea.'

She flew through the heavens to go and see Vertumnus, the handsome, hard-working god of changing seasons, growing plants and beautiful, peaceful gardens.

For a while, Pomona's life returned to normal. She dug the earth, she planted seedlings, she picked fruit. She was happy. But then the visitors, the would-be lovers, began to arrive again. All were young, and good-looking. All were friendly and eager. First came a harvester, hot and dusty from the fields. He offered Pomona baskets of ripe grain. She sent him away. Next, there was a hay-maker, carrying a long-handled scythe. He offered Pomona handfuls of sweet-smelling hay to protect her trees from frost in winter. She thanked him kindly, and sent him away. The third visitor was a ploughman, with mud from the fields on his boots. He offered to help dig her garden. 'That's heavy work,' he said. 'Yes it is, but I can manage fine,' replied Pomona. 'Now, please leave me in peace.' The last visitor staggered under the weight of a heavy wooden ladder. 'I made this for you,' he said. 'It will help us climb up to pick the apples from the topmost branches of your trees.'

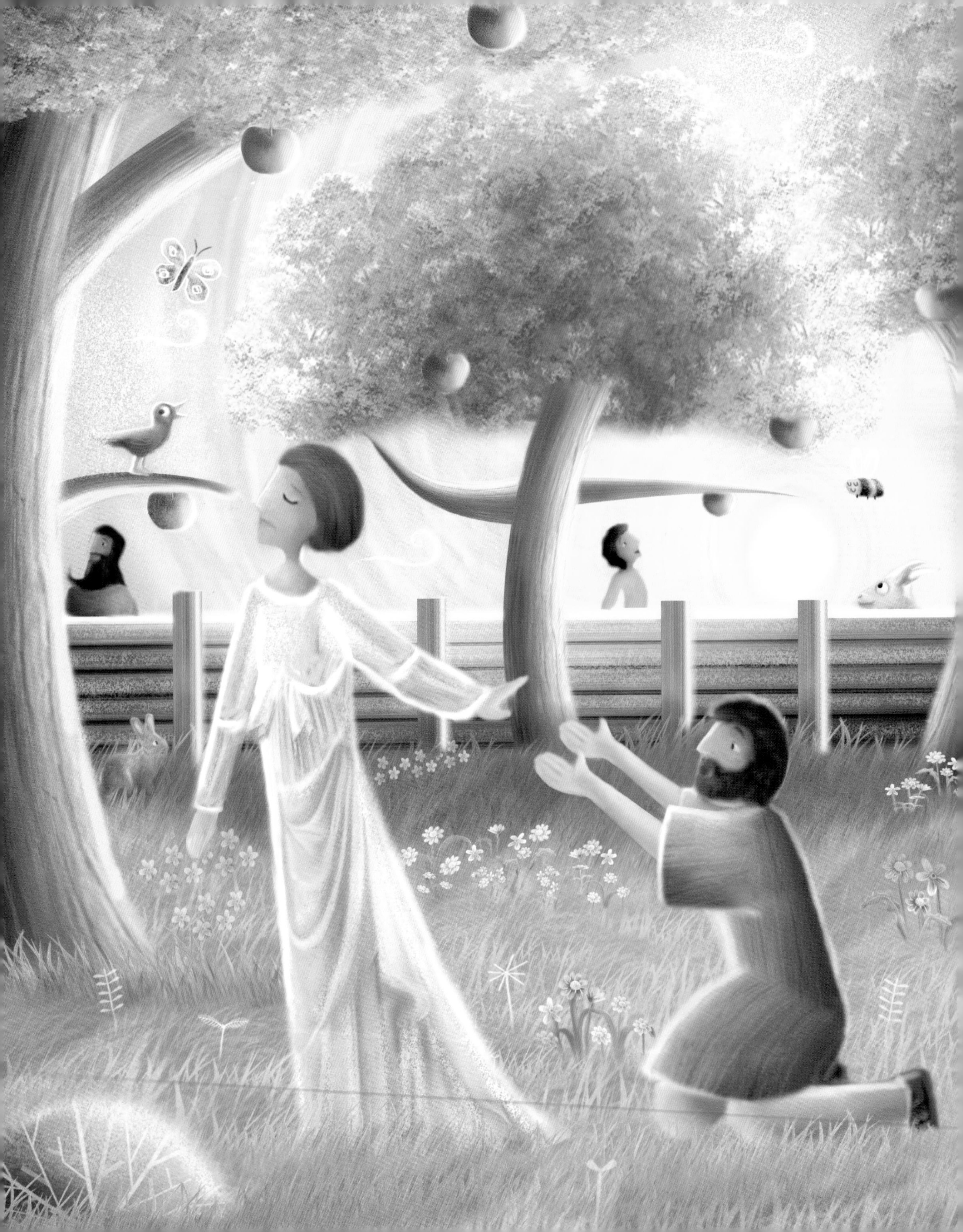

Enough was enough! 'Go away and stay away!' shouted Pomona. No 'please' or 'thank you' this time. The handsome would-be apple picker smiled, shrugged and walked away. But he left his ladder behind him.

Alone at last in her garden, Pomona had plenty of time to think. And the more she thought, the more suspicious she became. Where did all these young men come from, all of a sudden? Why did they all want to help her? Why did they praise her eyes, her smile, her hair, her figure (well, she knew the answer to that...)? But, she went on wondering, did all the young men know each other? Did anyone send them? Were their visits just by chance, or were they part of a plan?

There was no way she could think of to find the answers to those questions. She would just have to go on working in her garden, and wait and see.

It was a hot summer's day. The air was still, there was no sound apart from bees buzzing, and a heat haze shimmered across the leaves of Pomona's trees. She dipped her fingers in the stream that ran through her garden and let the cooling water trickle over them. Aaah! That was better!

But who was this, approaching the garden gate? Not another young man? No, it was a woman, and she was very, very old. She tottered along, supported by a strong stick. A shawl hid most of her face and shaded her head from the sun.

'Oh! Poor old lady!' cried Pomona. 'She looks exhausted!' She hurried to open the garden gate and led the old woman to a seat in the shade of her favourite fruit trees. 'Let me fetch you some water. And some fruit. That will refresh you.'

'Thank you, my dear,' the old woman replied. 'That is very kind.' And she ate and drank eagerly. The old lady seemed to fall asleep for a while, then she turned and spoke to Pomona.

'I feel much better now,' she said. 'Thank you

again for your kindness. But now, my dear, you must tell me a little about yourself. Do you live here alone? Do you care for this wonderful garden all by yourself? Do you have no-one to help you or admire you?'

They talked on and on, until the evening shadows lengthened on the grass and the air grew cool and sweet-smelling. The old lady certainly had a lot to say! She even told Pomona an old, old story, that

warned what happened when young girls refused to listen to a young man's words of love. It was a sad tale: the young man killed himself in despair, and, as a punishment, the goddess Venus turned the girl to stone.

'Surely that's not going to happen to me!' laughed Pomona. 'Now, honoured guest, can I pick a few more grapes for you? Or fetch some water?'

'No thank you,' said the old lady. And she went on talking, talking, talking about love.

Pomona did not know quite why, perhaps out of politeness to her visitor, or perhaps the goddess Venus was to blame, but she went on listening.

'I know just the husband for you,' the old lady was saying. 'Young Vertumnus. His task is to keep the seasons changing, year after year, and to make sure that all the living world obeys the laws of nature. He loves trees and gardens, too. You and he would work so well together...'

The old lady seemed surprisingly excited by what she was saying. She raised her hand to give extra force to her words. As she did so, her heavy shawl slipped and fell away from her face...

Yes, of course. You've guessed. The old lady was Vertumnus in disguise. And Vertumnus had been all the other visitors as well.

And yes, or so the ancient Roman story goes, Pomona married Vertumnus, and they lived very happily in her garden, working together through all the changing seasons of the year, for ever and ever.

HERCULES
AND THE
GIANT WHO SPAT FIRE

Hercules! Superman! Demigod! He fought monsters! He performed wondrous feats! And he was so manly that women were not allowed to enter his temple in case supernatural power surging from his statue made them pregnant (yes, really).

Hercules was worshipped as a hero by the ancient Romans and is still admired by strong men today. He used his strength to fight enemies of all kinds.

Here is a story the Romans told about Hercules

and a giant who once lived in Italy: the land that the Romans invaded, then conquered, then ruled.

Certainly, Cacus was not nice to know. The son of a volcano, or of the fire-god, Vulcan, Cacus was a giant; bigger and stronger than Hercules himself. Long before Rome was built, Cacus lived in a cave deep inside one of seven hills. He wrapped himself in poisonous snakes, spat deadly fire at his enemies, and had a cruel, scaly dragon perched on his shoulders. He ate only flesh, raw and dripping with blood, and his favourite food was humans. He cut off his victims' heads before eating their bodies, and hung them like nightmarish trophies at the entrance to his cave.

Hercules was born in Greece, but his adventures led him to many distant lands. After one long journey, he arrived in Italy. Tired and thirsty, he visited the temple of the goddess Fauna, and asked the priestess there to give him a drink. She refused, saying that the temple and its stores of food and water were for women only.

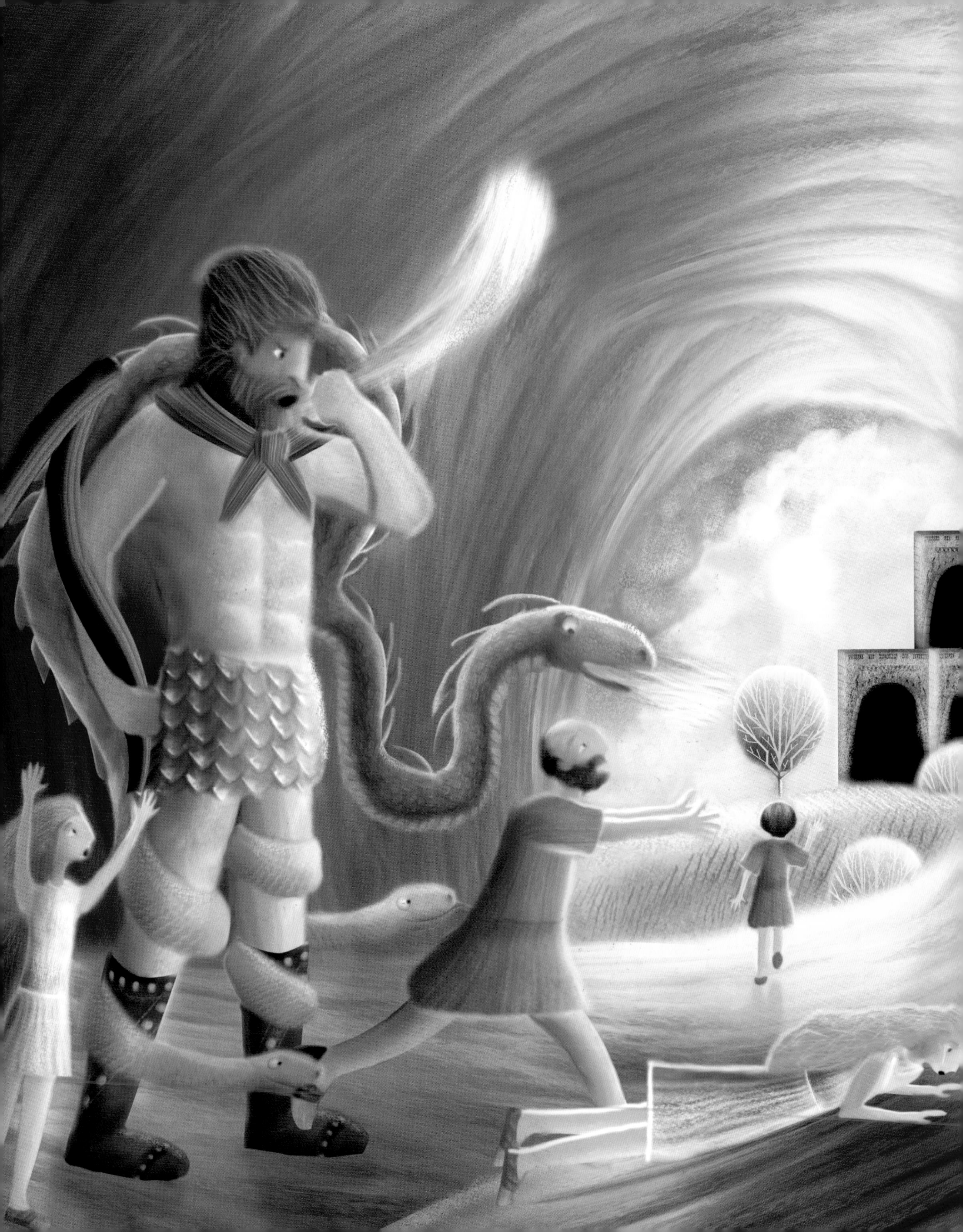

Hercules was shocked and offended. He stomped away in a rage.

'Stupid woman!' he snarled. 'I'll show her! I'll build a temple for men only, brave and bold men like me. It will be much bigger and better than her little female shrine. And...' he shook his fist towards the priestess, 'women will be banned!'

Temple-building is hard and heavy, even for a hero, but Hercules worked with a will. He made such an effort, grunting and groaning as he hoisted heavy loads, that he didn't notice Cacus creeping up behind him. Cacus wasn't planning to murder Hercules. Not yet, anyway. Instead, he had his eye on the herd of beautiful cattle that Hercules had just rescued from another monster, Geryon.

Carefully, and surprisingly quietly for so huge and heavy a creature, Cacus rounded up most of the cattle and led them away. He made them walk backwards by pulling them along by their tails. It was a clever trick, especially for a giant (they are usually said to be stupid). Anyone tracking the cattle's hoof-prints would go searching for them in the opposite direction. Cacus hid the cattle in his cave and began to get ready to kill one and enjoy a bloody feast.

Anyone else might have been fooled, but not Hercules. He led the few cattle that Cacus had not taken round and round the seven hills. Confused and fearful, they bellowed loud and long. An answering sound came from the stolen cattle trapped in Cacus's cave.

'Think you're clever?' sneered Cacus, standing at the cave doorway and spitting out flames and showers of sparks. 'A strong man, eh? Then come in and get your pretty cows. I dare you! Just try!'

He spat fire on his hands, which were huge as hams and hard as iron. He unwrapped his snakes and put his dragon carefully in a corner. Hercules put down the huge war club that he always carried and walked towards him.

What a fight! How they wrestled and stamped and kicked and punched and pummelled each other! The struggle lasted for hours. But at last Hercules managed to knock Cacus to the ground. Then he squeezed Cacus's neck so hard that the giant's eyes fell out. And that was how Cacus died.

When the farmers who lived on the seven hills heard the fight beginning, they left their fields and flocks of sheep and ran away to hide. A fight to the death between a superman and a giant was not safe to be near.

But now, was it really true? Had Cacus gone for ever? He had robbed and murdered for so long that no-one could remember a time when the countryside around the seven hills had been peaceful. But just one timid, shuddering look at the dead giant stretched out beside his cave was enough to reassure the farmers and their families. They were finally free from Cacus's terror.

Shouting with joy, the farmers crowded round Hercules, thanking him and offering him all their very best food, wine and treasure. Their wives and daughters draped him with garlands of laurel leaves, as worn by army commanders and Olympic champions. Hercules was their hero!

Many, many years later, a magnificent temple dedicated to Hercules stood at the heart of Rome. The Romans liked to say that Hercules himself had started the building. And also, the Romans added, linking past and present, the land where Hercules's beautiful cows once grazed was now the site of Rome's main cattle market.

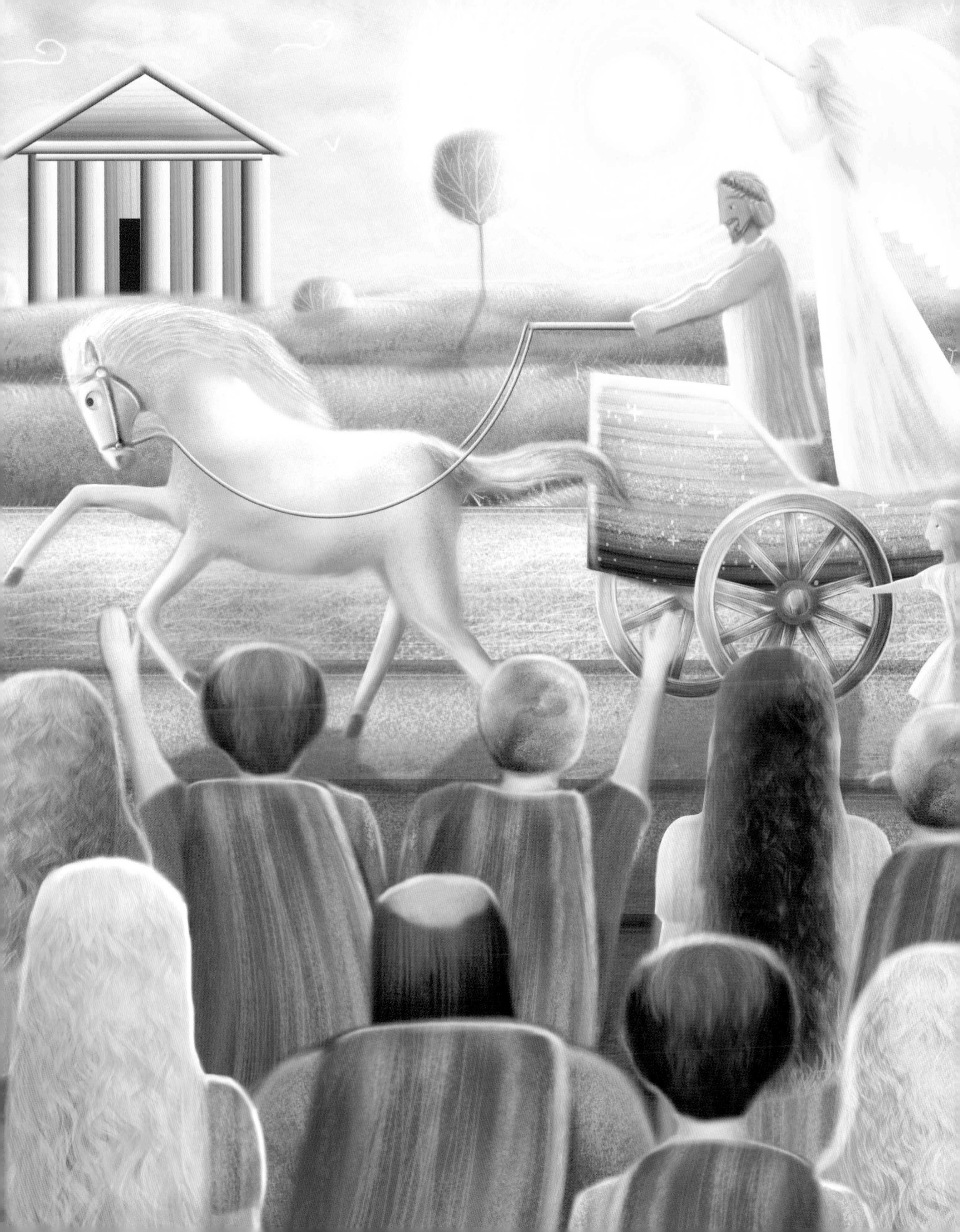

ARETHUSA – THE GIRL WHO GAVE WATER

Water, water everywhere. It falls as rain, swirls as mist and flows in deep, wide rivers. It trickles in sparkling streams and bubbles up from mysterious springs deep underground. Without water, there can be no life. That's why the Romans, and other ancient peoples, told so many stories about it.

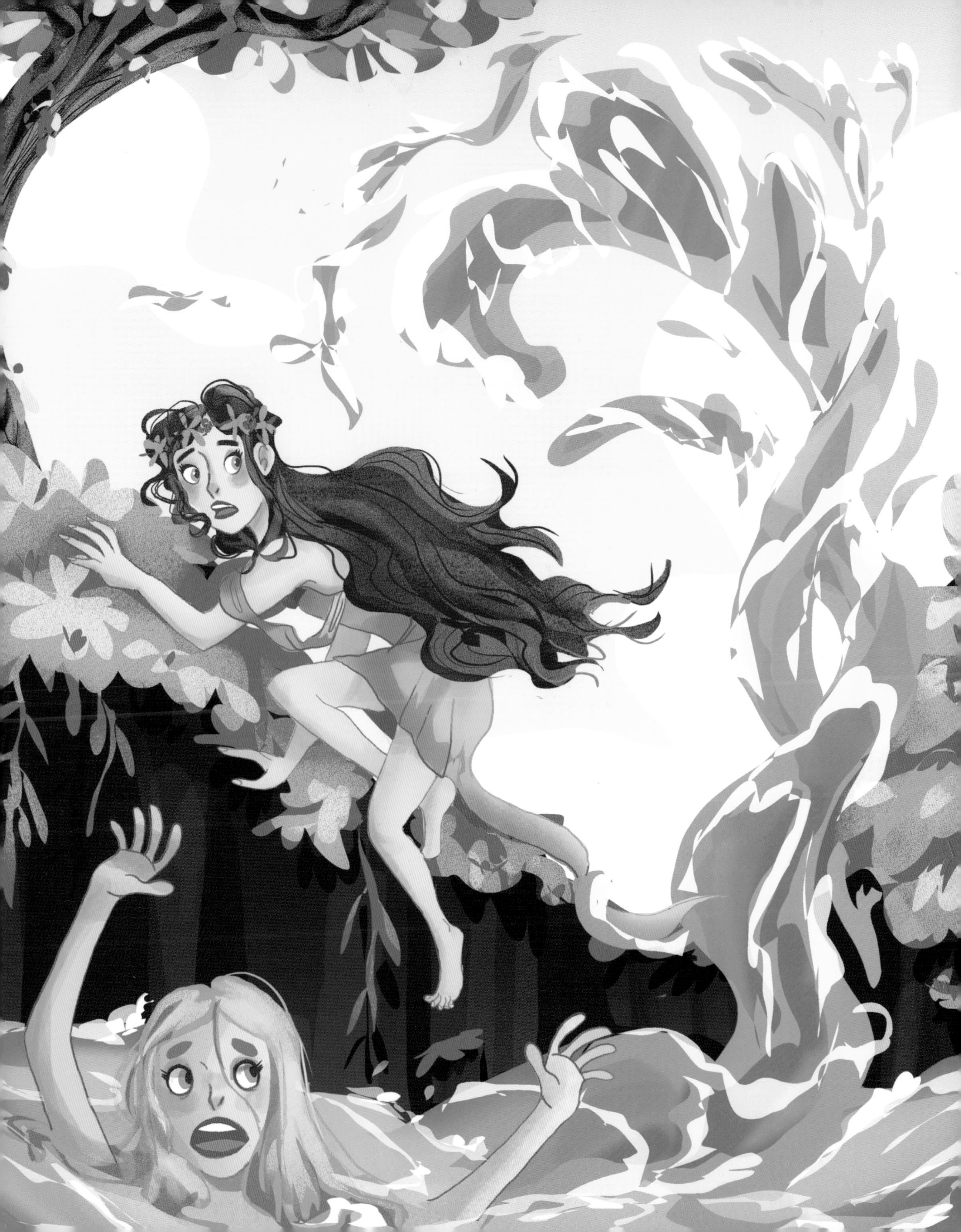

In the beginning, so people said, the whole world was full of unseen forces. Everything that existed had a spirit living in it. There were spirits of rocks and woods and mountains and meadows. And spirits of water in all its different disguises. Sometimes these spirits were honoured as gods; sometimes they were feared as ghosts or demons. Most were friendly and helpful – to humans, as well as to each other. But a few were very dangerous.

Arethusa was a spirit who lived, wild and free, with her companions in the forest. One day, when they all felt tired and hot and dusty after hunting, they came to the bank of a river that flowed through a forest glade. How cool its waters looked! How inviting!

One by one, Arethusa and her friends scrambled down into the river. Together, they splashed and swam and floated, while the river water gently washed and refreshed them. Then they clambered up the steep river bank, and stretched out on a soft, grassy meadow to dry themselves in the Sun.

All, that is, except Arethusa. The water was so cool and pleasant that she didn't want to leave. She floated lightly, on her back, gazing up at flickering patterns of sunlight as a gentle breeze fluttered the leaves of the overhanging trees.

But what's happening now? The river waters are swirling and churning! It's as if a giant hand is stirring them round and round. They heave and bubble. They roll and belch. Arethusa's companions, safe on land, run away in terror. But poor Arethusa? What can she do? She's trapped in the water!

Now, look again. Who's this? The waters have calmed down and a tall and terrifying man is standing in the middle of the river. It's Alpheus, a spirit, or perhaps a god, and this river belongs to him!

'I love you, Arethusa!' he cries, and his voice is rough and urgent, like a torrent rushing over pebbles in a river bed.

'Come and be my bride. Then you can stay with me and live in the water for ever!'

Arethusa was horrified. Fearing that Alpheus would seize her and drag her under the water, she whispered a desperate prayer to the mighty goddess Diana.

'Dear, honoured goddess! Please, please save me! You protect unmarried girls, and people who love hunting. And you're the guardian of the forests...'

High in the sky, riding a crescent moon, Diana heard Arethusa. Straight away she sent a cloud of swirling mist, to hide Arethusa from Alpheus. Safe inside, Arethusa swam to the bank, climbed out of the river and started to run through the forest. Alpheus followed, but every time he tried to grab Arethusa, Diana worked her magic and Alpheus was left clutching at handfuls of nothing more than damp cloud.

Arethusa ran on, until, she felt sure, the goddess Diana was telling her to stop and rest for a while. Gasping with fear, she leaned up against a tree to catch her breath. Anxiously, she looked all around. Yes, that was Alpheus, over there. He was still chasing her!

Arethusa slumped back against her tree. She was utterly, utterly exhausted. She didn't have the strength to keep on running. Surely, Alpheus would catch her now?

Arethusa's knees bent. Her shoulders sagged. Her whole body slumped downwards. And, as this happened, a crack opened up in the rocky ground beneath her feet. At the same time she was changed, transformed. No longer a free spirit or a misty cloud, she became a lively, fast-flowing stream of crystal-clear water. She plunged down and down and down, deep into the earth. Alpheus looked on, helpless.

The water was Arethusa; Arethusa was the water. Now she was happy and free. Her spring flowed on underground, through caves and channels hidden in the rock, until it came back to the surface on the tiny island of Ortygia, bubbling up to fill a deep, dark pool.

For the first time ever, thanks to Arethusa, there was water on Ortygia, and soon there were trees and flowers and animals and birds. For the first time, people could live on the island, and grow crops and build houses. They praised Arethusa and her water. They begged her to go on living with them on the island. And, so they say, she lives there still.

Arethusa brought water, but she also brought much more. She brought life itself.

GLOSSARY

Ancestors
Relatives who have lived before you.

Chasm
A deep crack in the earth's surface.

Demigod
Half man, half god.

Descendants
Relatives who live after you.

Fury
Goddess of anger and revenge.

Hesperides
Legendary land at the west end of the Mediterranean Sea.

Oracle
Person who spoke words believed to come from the gods.

Pious
Respectful of ancestors and gods.

Sacrifice
Offering made to a god or goddess.

Scythe
Farm tool for cutting corn; a curved blade on a long pole.

Thrace
Region in south-east Europe (now parts of Bulgaria, Greece and Turkey).

Trojans
People from Troy, a great city in Asia Minor (now Turkey).